THIS BOOK BELONGS TO

T H E
Christmas Bear

BY **Henrietta Stickland** ✳ ILLUSTRATED BY **Paul Stickland**

BACK**PACK**BOOKS
·
NEW YORK

Cub lived at the top of the world with his mother and father. One Christmas Eve, he left his den and went exploring. He followed his nose, over a hill and across the snow. It led him to a big, bright hole. Who lives down there? Cub wondered.

Cub followed his nose farther and farther, until all of a sudden . . .

he fell in!
Down . . .

down . . .

down he fell.

Bump! Cub landed at the bottom. When he peeked through his paws, he saw that he had landed in a cozy study—right next to Santa Claus!

"How kind of you to drop in," said Santa, in spite of his surprise. "You must be answering my ad for a helper. Good! Let me show you what we do here." Cub was very excited.

"This is the mail room," said Santa. "We receive letters from children all over the world. Do you speak many languages? We must always make sure that the right present gets to each child."

Cub shook his head sadly. He knew how to speak only one language.

"Next we have the workshops, where all the toys are made to order. Dolls, trains, puzzles, games, spaceships . . . every kind of toy in the world. I've designed some of them myself," Santa said.

Cub especially liked the dinosaurs. The purple ones seemed almost as if they were alive.

Then Santa Claus took Cub into a gigantic room full of noisy machinery.

"This is the North Pole itself," he shouted over the din. "Here we make our own electricity. You can see it's actually quite simple."

Cub nodded, but he wasn't sure he really understood!

"This might be the perfect job for you," Santa said in the next room. "This is the testing room. Would you like to test some toys for me?"

Cub was happy to test toy after toy. They were all in tip-top shape. But he liked the bears best. "Ready to see some more?" asked Santa.

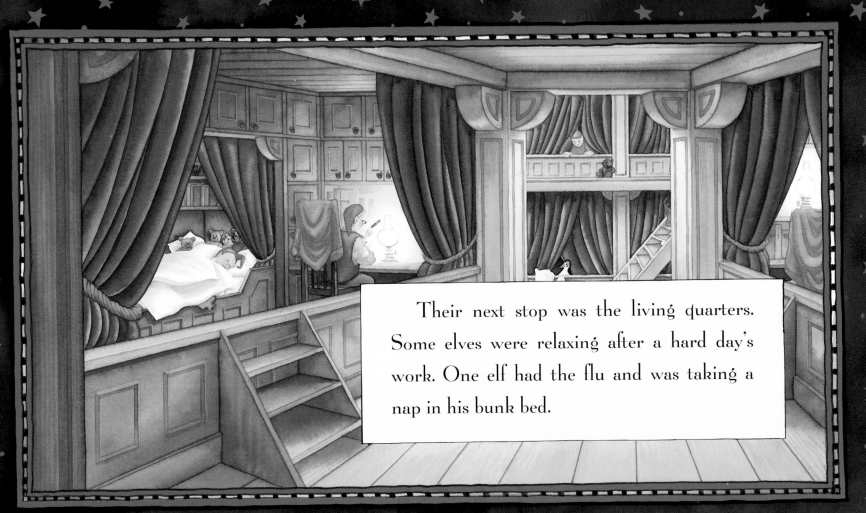

Their next stop was the living quarters. Some elves were relaxing after a hard day's work. One elf had the flu and was taking a nap in his bunk bed.

"Time for a snack," Santa suggested as they went through the kitchen. "I bet you'd like some fish and ice cream."

"Yes, please," Cub said. "Thank you, Santa."

"Back to work again," said Santa, taking Cub to the storeroom. Elves were busy with last-minute tasks, crossing items off lists and addressing packages.

Cub tried to get a closer look. Was one of these presents for him?

Downstairs in the wrapping room, huge bolts of shiny paper hung from the ceiling. Toys of all shapes and sizes passed through the wrapping machines while the elves watched carefully.

Cub saw that big sacks stuffed with presents were being lowered into the stables. "We can go down, too," Santa said.

"Well, little Cub, do you like our new kittens?"

Cub nodded. "I like the mice, too."

"I think it's almost time to go," Santa continued. "The reindeer are ready. But before we leave, I have to tell you a secret. I know that you did not really come to be my helper.

"But don't worry! I just think your parents might want you home for Christmas. I can take you in my sleigh, if you like."

"Oh, yes!" said Cub.

"And before I forget," Santa added, taking a present from the pile, "here is a special one, just for you. And now, first stop, the top of the world!"

In the blink of an eye, Cub was home.

"Thank you for your help, Cub," said Santa. "Remember— you'll always be my Christmas Bear. Merry Christmas!"

"Merry Christmas, Santa," said Cub's mother. "And now, little Cub, it's time for bed."

So Cub curled up next to the best Christmas presents of all.

For Emily, Little Etta, Katie, Danda,
Erica, Thomas, and Katharine, with much love
H. S.

For my grampa, artist and illustrator
Geoffrey Squire
P. S.

Typography by Adrian Leichter

2006 Backpack Books

ISBN-13: 978-0-7607-8417-4
ISBN-10: 0-7607-8417-5

Printed and bound in China

1 3 5 7 9 10 8 6 4 2